HEADS

HEADS
Ron and Nancy Goor

Atheneum   1988   New York

With love, to Alex and Dan

Atheneum
Macmillan Publishing Company
866 Third Avenue, New York, NY 10022
Collier Macmillan Canada, Inc.
First Edition
Printed in the United States of America

10 9 8 7 6 5 4 3 2 1

Library of Congress Cataloging-in-Publication Data
Goor, Ron.
Heads/by Ron and Nancy Goor.—1st ed.
p.   cm.
Summary: Compares and contrasts the characteristics of the eyes,
ears, nose, and mouth of a variety of animals.
ISBN 0-689-31400-0
1. Senses and sensation—Juvenile literature.   2. Head—Juvenile
literature.   3. Animals—Miscellanea—Juvenile literature.
[1. Senses and sensation.   2. Heads.   3. Animals—Miscellanea.]
I. Goor, Nancy.   II. Title.
QP434.G66 1988
599′ .01042—dc19
87-30262 CIP AC

HEADS

Your **head** has **eyes** for seeing

and **ears** for hearing

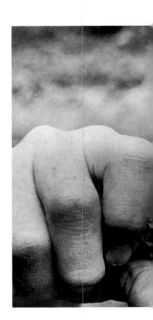

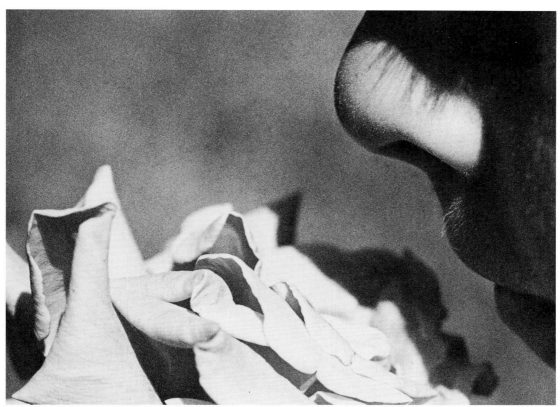

a **nose** for smelling

a **mouth** for tasting,
    eating, and talking.

Your nose, mouth, eyes, and ears help you to know and live in your world.

Other animals also have eyes, ears, noses, and mouths to help them know the world around them and to survive—
to find their way,
to find and catch food,
to escape from enemies,
and to find mates in the different kinds of places where they live.

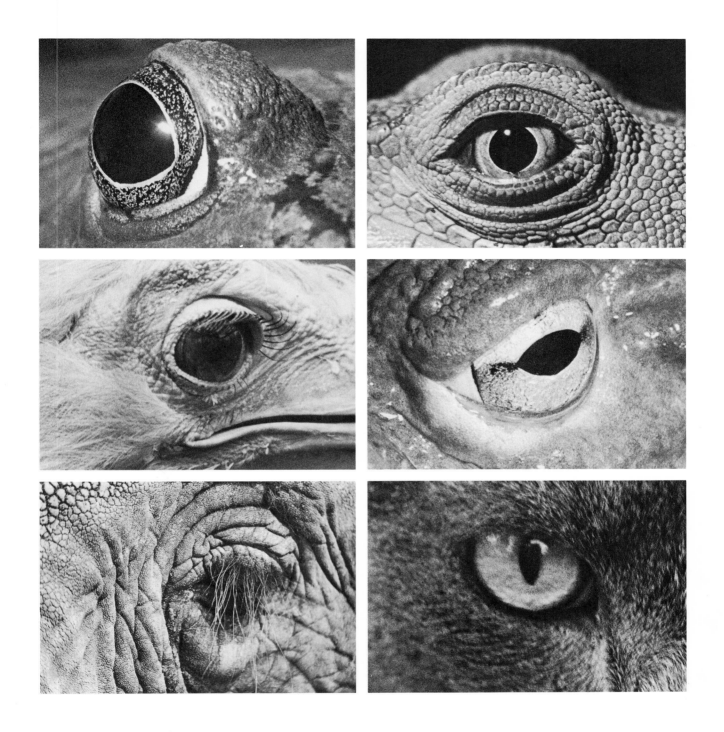

EYES

Animals have different kinds of eyes for living in different places.

9

10

Hawks and eagles have large, tube-shaped eyes that work like telescopes. As they fly high above the ground they can spot their dinner—a tiny mouse, a fish—hundreds of feet below. Hawks can see eight times as far away as you or I. They have the best eyesight of all living animals.

Gavials, long-nosed crocodiles, live and hunt in shallow water. Their eyes are on top of their head so they can peer out above the water while their body is hidden below. Out of sight, under the water, their long snout hangs open while they wait for a meal to swim by. Gavials can keep their eyes open under water, too. Their inner lids are like see-through window shades. The lids slide across their eyes to protect them under water.

13

These animals also live in shallow water and have eyes on the top of their head.

Pottos are small animals that are related to monkeys, apes, and man. They live in the rain forests of West Africa. Their round, unblinking eyes are enormous. During the day, when the sun is bright, the part of the eye that lets in light—the iris—closes down and the potto does not see well. In the evening, when the light is dim, the iris opens wide and the potto can easily see small insects and birds to catch and eat.

Some animals have eyes specially placed to help them hunt their prey.

Tigers' eyes face forward on their heads. Because both eyes work together to see the same thing, cats can see in depth. They can judge how far away an animal is. They watch very carefully as they stalk their prey and know just when to pounce.

Some animals have eyes specially placed to warn them of danger.

Zebras live on the open grasslands of Africa. They have many enemies—lions, cheetahs, and wild dogs. They stand still like statues so they will not attract attention. With eyes on the sides of their head, they can look to the front, to the side, and behind without moving. When they see an enemy, they run away very fast.

These are the eyes of animals that hunt.

These are the eyes of animals that are hunted.

21

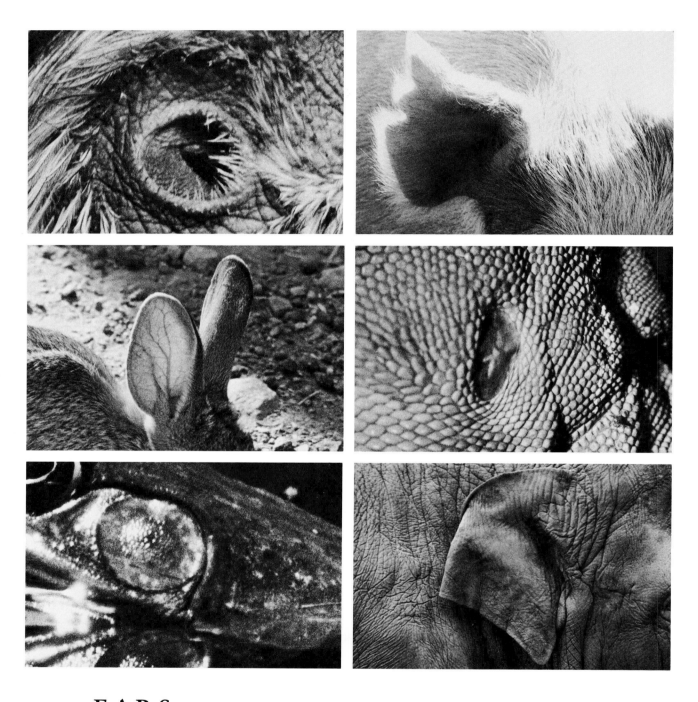

E A R S

Animals have different kinds of ears to live different kinds of
lives. Some use their ears to help them get around or listen for
danger. Some use their ears to help them find food.

Insect-eating bats fly at night. They use sound to keep from bumping into things and to catch insects as they fly in the dark. Bats send out high-pitched sounds from their mouth or nostrils. The sound hits an object and the echo bounces back. Bat ears are specially shaped to receive the echo. Bats can tell where an object is, its size, and shape by its echo. This is called *echolocation*.

African elephants have the largest ears of all animals. Because they do not see well, they stretch out their tremendous ears to catch sounds of danger. They also stretch out their ears to look even bigger and more scary to a lion stalking their young. Elephants' ears help them keep cool. Heat leaves their bodies through the many blood vessels just below the skin of their ears. Elephant ears also make handy fans.

24

African desert foxes, or fennecs, have ears that seem too large for their bodies. But these oversized ears help them live in the hot desert. During the day fennecs sleep in sand burrows to hide from the burning sun. Heat escaping from the surface of their large ears cools them. Fennecs hunt when the sun goes down. They need excellent hearing to hunt in the dark. Their large ears collect sounds—even very quiet sounds—of animals to catch and eat.

Rhinos live on the open plains of Africa. They are so nearsighted, they are nearly blind. But they hear very well. Their ears swivel around in all directions to locate sounds. When a rhino hears a noise, it gets scared and charges. Sometimes one will charge a Land Rover van by mistake.

These animals also live on the open plains and have ears that swivel to catch sounds. When they hear a noise of danger, they run away fast.

27

Some animals use their ears to help them locate mates.

Male frogs call female frogs by making a booming sound. When they blow up the sac beneath their chin with air, their croaks sound louder. The sound can be heard more than a mile away. The ears of frogs are made of thin skin that vibrates like the top of a drum. Female frogs find males by listening for their mating calls.

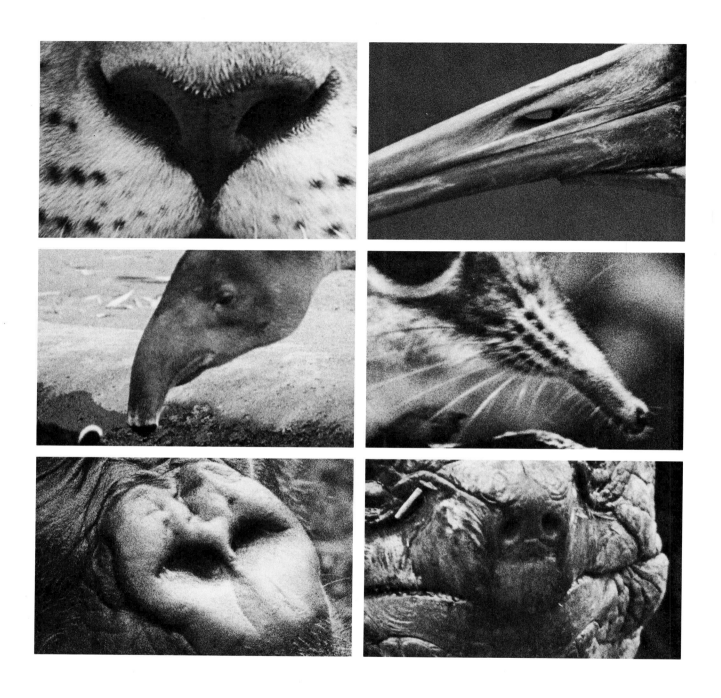

NOSES
Animals have different types of noses to help them live in different ways.

30

Some animals use their noses to warn them of danger or to find food.

Deer stand very still and sniff into the wind. They are checking for the scent of hungry animals on the hunt. But if the hunter is downwind, the deer will not detect its smell. Animals that hunt often stalk their prey so their scent won't be blown toward the prey's sensitive nose.

31

Hippos live in shallow water. Their nostrils are located on the top of their long, broad snouts. Their nostrils stick up above the water so hippos can breathe while their bodies are hidden underneath. They smell the air for danger.

With their heads under water, hippos look like big, gray rocks. Hippos close their nostrils when they go completely underwater. They can hold their breath for six minutes at a time. When one comes to the surface it blows out the air with a snort so loud it can be heard miles away.

Anteaters cannot see or hear very well. They use their keen sense of smell to find ants and termites. They poke their long, narrow snouts into anthills and termite mounds. They lick up thousands of ants or termites with their long, sticky tongues.

Some noses are used like tools.

Pigs have snouts that are flat like shovels. They root around the earth for bulbs, fungi, roots, and earthworms. A pig's nose is very sensitive to smells. Pigs are used in France to sniff out special mushrooms called truffles that grow underground.

An elephant's trunk is like a powerful arm. Its forty thousand
muscles and tendons give it great strength and control. It can
pick up a six-hundred-pound tree. It can knock down enemies.
The tip of the trunk has "fingers" to pluck leaves or fruit from
a tree. The African elephant has two fingers at the end of its
trunk; the Indian elephant has one. Elephants' trunks are like
gigantic straws for sucking water in and like gigantic hoses for
spraying water out.

Some animals use their noses to attract mates. Some use their noses to scare other males.

Each December, male elephant seals come to the beaches of California. These elephant seal bulls are very large. They may be sixteen feet long. They may weigh six thousand pounds. They fight with each other for space on the beach. Males force air through their noses to make tremendous bellowing sounds. These sounds scare other males away. Females come to the beach later. They prefer males who have won the most land on the beach. Females may also be attracted to the male with the biggest nose!

38

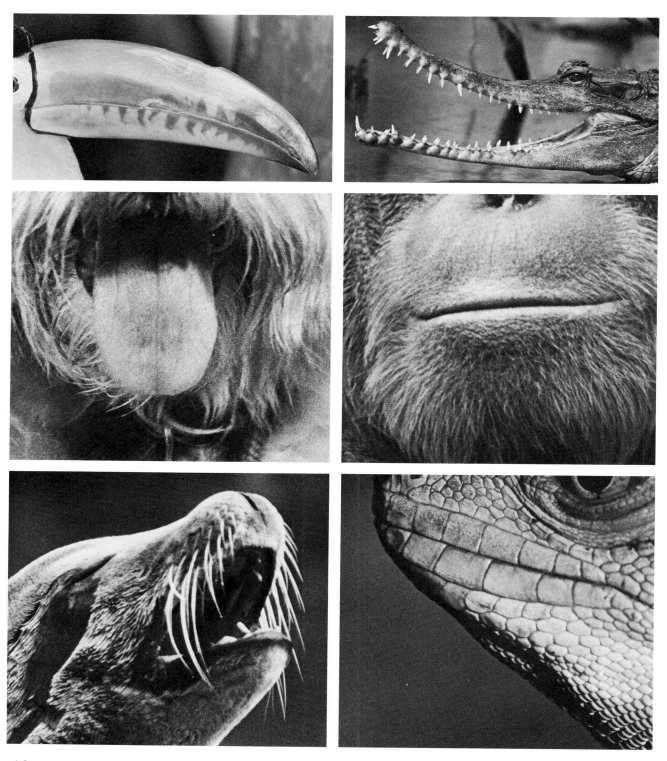

MOUTHS

Animals have specially shaped mouths to catch or gather food in the different places they live.

Alligator snapping turtles lie very still on river bottoms. Their heads and bodies are covered with algae. They look like lumps of mud blanketed with dead leaves. To catch food, an alligator snapping turtle opens its mouth wide. Its tongue wriggles just like a worm. A fish swims into the turtle's mouth to eat the "worm." Snap! The alligator snapping turtle closes its jaws and eats the fish.

41

Giraffes like to eat the leaves and flowers of mimosa trees. A giraffe wraps its eighteen-inch-long tongue around a high branch. It pulls the branch to its mouth. Hard little bumps called papillae cover the tongue and make it grip like sandpaper. The giraffe grabs off leaves and flowers with its lips. Mimosa trees have sharp thorns but they do not harm giraffes. The lining of a giraffe's mouth is coated with thick saliva to protect it against the thorns.

The white rhinoceros and the black rhinoceros have different lips
because they live in different places and eat different foods. The
black rhinoceros lives in East Africa where shrubs and low-
growing trees cover the dry land. Its upper lip is made to wrap
around twigs and grab off leaves to eat. The white rhinoceros
lives on the plains of South and Central Africa and eats grasses.
Its upper lip is wide and flat at the bottom for grazing.

44

45

Beaks are bird's lips. They use their beaks to get food. You can figure out what a bird eats by the size and shape of its beak.

Parrots are seed eaters. Their beaks are thick and heavy to crack seeds.

Woodpeckers use their narrow, sharp beaks to peck holes in trees. They use their long, thin tongues to pull out insects.

Ducks have beaks like shovels to scoop up mud and sift through it to find food.

Eagles, hawks, vultures, and owls have sharp, hooked beaks to tear their food apart.

Flamingos lower their heads
and hold their curved beaks
upside down in the water.
Their tongues move very fast
to pull in water and mud and
push them out again. Fringes
on the edge of their beaks
strain out tiny animals from
the muddy water for them
to eat.

50

Some animals use their mouths to detect chemicals in the air that alert them to food or danger.

When lions yawn, they are not tired. They are testing the air for the smell of other animals. Perhaps they smell an animal that will become a meal. Perhaps they smell an animal that might hurt their young.

Some animals use their sharp teeth to capture and kill their prey.

Crocodiles lie in the shallow waters of swamps and marshes. Only their eyes and nostrils show above the water. They look like floating logs. When an animal comes too close, a crocodile grabs it with its strong jaws and pulls it under water to drown it. Crocodile teeth are used to hold prey, not to chew it. Crocodiles tear their victims apart and gulp them down in big lumps.

52

These animals also use their teeth for attack.

Many animals use their teeth to protect them from enemies.

When a hippo is threatened, it opens its mouth wide. Two long
canine teeth stick out of the lower jaw. These sharp teeth look
like elephant tusks. They make powerful weapons. In fact,
hippos have been known to bite large crocodiles in two. When
a hippo closes its mouth, these teeth fit into pockets in the
upper jaw. Hippos' bad breath may also help keep
enemies away!

54

These animals also use their long canine teeth for defense.

HEADS

All the parts of an animal's head—the eyes, ears, nose, and mouth—work together to help it live in its world.

Owls live in forests. They hunt at night. They must use all the parts of their head to survive. Their huge eyes gather light to help them see in the dark. Like us, owls see straight ahead with both eyes. The vision from each eye overlaps in the center so they can judge distances. This helps owls catch small animals that move fast. Owls must hear well to hunt in the dark. A small earflap at a different level on each side of its head helps an owl locate sounds. Owls' beaks are sharp and curved to rip prey apart.

Dromedary camels live in the deserts of North Africa. Their heads are made for living in hot, dry deserts where strong winds blow sand everywhere. A double row of long lashes keeps sand out of their eyes. Tufts of hair keep sand out of their ears. Muscles tightly close the camel's long, thin nostrils against the biting wind. Food is scarce in the desert. A camel's lips and tongue are tough so it can chew thorny desert plants. A camel's upper lip is split to help it grasp whatever food it can find.

62

Sea lions live along the Pacific coasts of North America, South America, and Australia. Their heads are made for living in water. They are streamlined for fast swimming and diving. Sea lions can stay underwater for up to twenty minutes—sometimes twelve hundred feet below the surface. The pupils of their eyes are very large to let in light when they fish deep in the dark oceans. Their nostrils and ears close tight to keep out water. But sea lions can still hear under water. Vibrations from sounds are conducted by the water through their ear walls to their brains. Sea lions may also use their whiskers to "hear." Some scientists think that sea lions send out clicking sounds to locate food. The sound bounces off objects and is picked up by the sea lions' sensitive whiskers. Sea lions' teeth are sharp, but not for chewing. They grab onto slippery fish and then swallow them whole.

When a sea lion mother nuzzles her baby, she is not just being affectionate. She is remembering its smell. Her sense of smell is so good, she can find her young among the thousands of sea lions living together on one beach.

Animals live in forests, mountains, plains, deserts, and seas. They fly in the sky. They climb through the jungles and burrow through the earth. An animal's eyes, ears, nose, and mouth work together to help it find its way, locate and eat food, escape from enemies, and find a mate in the different places where it lives.

Animals not named in the text (left to right, top to bottom)
P. 9 American bullfrog, green-crested basilisk (lizard), secretary bird, African bullfrog, African elephant, house cat; p. 10 black eagle; p. 11 white-breasted sea eagle; p. 14 American bullfrog, hippopotamus, American alligator; p. 20 lion, timber wolf, house cat; p. 21 ostrich, prairie dog, gazelle; p. 22 rhea, pig, rabbit, green-crested basilisk, bullfrog, Indian elephant; p. 27 Thomson's gazelles, gnu, zebra; p. 28 American bullfrog; p. 30 jaguar, white-naped crane, tapir, elephant shrew, gorilla, tortoise; p. 40 toucan, gavial, dog, orangutan, sea lion, green-crested basilisk; p. 47 vulture, falcon, eagle, owl; p. 55 peccary, sloth bear, giant panda; p. 56 orangutan, squirrel, iguana, boa constrictor; p. 57 armadillo, red kangaroo, bongo (antelope), crowned crane.